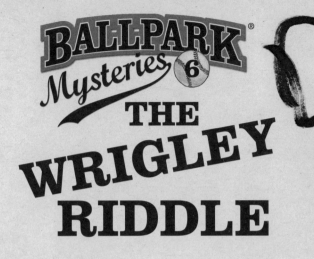

BALLPARK
Mysteries 6
THE
WRIGLEY
RIDDLE

BALLPARK® Mysteries 6

THE WRIGLEY RIDDLE

by David A. Kelly

illustrated by Mark Meyers

A STEPPING STONE BOOK™

Random House 🏠 New York

To Zack Hample, author of The Baseball *and the best ballhawk I know—6,413 balls and counting —D.A.K.*

To Aaron, Kati, and family. Thanks for the inspiration and for showing me what a pencil can do. —M.M.

"It's a great day for a ball game; let's play two."
—Ernie "Mr. Cub" Banks, Chicago Cubs shortstop

This is a work of fiction. Names, characters, places, and incidents either are the product of the author's imagination or are used fictitiously. Any resemblance to actual persons, living or dead, events, or locales is entirely coincidental.

Text copyright © 2013 by David A. Kelly
Cover art and interior illustrations copyright © 2013 by Mark Meyers

All rights reserved. Published in the United States by Random House Children's Books, a division of Random House LLC, a Penguin Random House Company, New York.

Random House and the colophon are registered trademarks and A Stepping Stone Book and the colophon are trademarks of Random House LLC. Ballpark Mysteries® is a registered trademark of Upside Research, Inc.

Visit us on the Web!
SteppingStonesBooks.com
randomhouse.com/kids

Educators and librarians, for a variety of teaching tools, visit us at
RHTeachersLibrarians.com

Library of Congress Cataloging-in-Publication Data
Kelly, David A. (David Andrew)
The Wrigley riddle / by David A. Kelly ; illustrated by Mark Meyers. — 1st ed.
p. cm. — (Ballpark mysteries ; 6)
"A Stepping Stone Book."
Summary: During a visit to the Chicago Cubs' Wrigley Field, cousins Mike and Kate investigate why someone has been tampering with the famous ivy vines growing on the outfield walls. Includes historical note.
ISBN 978-0-307-97776-2 (pbk.) — ISBN 978-0-307-97777-9 (lib. bdg.) — ISBN 978-0-307-97778-6 (ebook)
[1. Baseball—Fiction. 2. Cousins—Fiction. 3. Buried treasure—Fiction. 4. Wrigley Field (Chicago, Ill.)—Fiction. 5. Chicago (Ill.)—Fiction. 6. Mystery and detective stories.]
I. Meyers, Mark, ill. II. Title.
PZ7.K2936Wri 2013 [Fic]—dc23 2012010244

Printed in the United States of America
11 10 9 8 7

Contents

Trouble with Ivy

"Heads up!" Mike Walsh called from the top of Wrigley Field's bleacher seats. His cousin Kate Hopkins stood at the bottom, near the first row. It was three hours before the game, so the stadium was mostly empty.

Mike fired a fastball down to Kate. She reached up to catch it, but the throw was high. The ball sailed straight into the outfield.

"Oh no!" Kate cried.

THWAP! The ball bounced off the foot of Louie Lopez, the Chicago Cubs' star center fielder.

"*¡Huy!*" Louie exclaimed. "What's that?"

Mike's freckled face blushed. "Sorry!" he called out. "I was playing catch with my cousin. I threw the ball a little too high." Mike ran down the steps to where Kate stood by the short green wall that overlooked the outfield.

Louie shook his head. "More like a *lot* too high," he said with a smile. "I know our fans like to throw the other team's home runs back. But this is the first time I've seen a fan throw his *own* ball onto the field."

"I guess I'm stronger than I knew," Mike said. He flexed his muscles, pretending to be a muscleman.

Kate rolled her eyes. "It's not about strength," she said. "You're not going to make the major leagues if you can't aim better!"

Mike ignored her. He leaned over the outfield wall. Dark green ivy leaves covered the entire side. "Where did it go?" he asked Kate.

Kate shrugged. "Into the ivy, I think."

"Aunt Laura, can we come get my baseball?" he asked Kate's mom.

Mrs. Hopkins was standing in center field with Louie Lopez. Her short curly hair poked out from under a blue Cooperstown baseball cap. She wore a black messenger bag over her shoulder and scribbled notes on a pad.

"Not right now. I have to finish interviewing Louie by the time batting practice starts," Kate's mother said. "You can get the ball when I'm done."

Kate's mom was a reporter for the website American Sportz. She was writing a story on Louie Lopez and the Cubs' recent winning streak. Mike, Kate, and Mrs. Hopkins had taken a train to Chicago from Cooperstown, New York, the day before. Mike and Kate lived down the street from each other in

Cooperstown, near the Baseball Hall of Fame. They went to games with Kate's mom whenever they could.

"Cool!" Mike said. "Hey, Kate, did you notice the scoreboard yet?" He pointed to the scoreboard. It was wedged into the back corner of the park, towering over rows of bleacher seats.

"It's huge," Mike said. "I read that no one's ever hit a home run into it."

"They haven't!" said a voice.

Kate and Mike turned to see a man walking down the bleacher steps. He had a short black crew cut and wore a shiny blue Cubs warm-up jacket.

"I'm Paul Thomas, media director for the Cubs. Your mom wanted me to say hello," he said. "Mike's right. No home run has hit the scoreboard yet. But we get plenty of balls that disappear into the ivy down there."

4

"It's kind of weird that a baseball park has ivy growing all over the outfield wall," Kate said. "Doesn't it mess up the players?"

"Our players *love* the ivy. Wrigley Field just

wouldn't be the same without it," Mr. Thomas said. "P. K. Wrigley had the ivy planted and the scoreboard built in 1937. His family owned the Chicago Cubs. They also owned a big chewing gum company. That's why Wrigley Field has the same name as the gum."

"Then why don't home runs *stick* to the scoreboard?" Mike asked. He winked at Kate. "Get it? Gum. Stick?"

"Ouch! That's bad," Mr. Thomas said. "You'll have to let me *chew* on that for a while. . . ."

Kate groaned.

"Okay, enough." Mr. Thomas held up his hands in surrender. "Your mother's almost done with her Louie Lopez interview. I'll take you to the field."

Kate and Mike followed Mr. Thomas down some stairs to a hallway under the bleachers. The gates had opened and fans were starting to come in. They passed a food cart and turned into a long, narrow room filled with shovels, grass seed, and chalk.

"What's this room for?" Kate asked.

"It's the groundskeepers' room," Mr. Thomas said. "Maybe you'll meet Mr. Lee later."

On the other side of the room, Mr. Thomas led them through a door onto the grassy outfield.

"Wow, Kate! Look at this!" Mike cried.

Wrigley Field spread out before them like a ballpark from a postcard. Two green ribbons of seats wrapped around the field, from first base to third. The famous ivy-covered outfield wall rose up just behind where they stood. Beyond the wall were the bleacher seats. The giant green-and-white scoreboard rose from the pyramid of bleachers. Here and there, workers were setting up for the day's game.

Louie Lopez waved them over. "I know you can use some work on throwing, but are you any good at hitting?" he asked Mike.

"You bet I am," Mike said, nodding. "I hit a double in Little League last week."

"Well, how about you and Kate stop by the

batting cage under the bleachers tomorrow morning. I need to work on my swing to keep our eleven-game winning streak alive," Louie said. "But I can let you two take some swings as well."

"Sounds great!" Kate said. "I'll bet I hit more than Mike does!"

"No way," Mike replied. "But if you do, I'll hit them farther!"

"We'll see about that," Kate said. Then she thanked Louie, saying, "*Muchas gracias,* Señor Lopez." Kate was teaching herself Spanish. She tried to speak it whenever she had a chance.

"Call me Louie," he said. He tipped his cap to Kate, Mike, and Mrs. Hopkins and sauntered off the field.

Mrs. Hopkins put away her notepad and checked her watch. "I have to head back to the pressroom," she said. "You two want to come?"

"Wait! I need to find my baseball," Mike said. He jogged over to the right-field wall. "I know it's here somewhere."

"You're looking in the wrong spot," Kate called. She went to the center of the wall and scanned the area for Mike's shiny white baseball. "I think it's over here."

The outfield wall was about twelve feet high and ran from one side of the park to the other. It was covered top to bottom in leafy green ivy vines. The vines were so thick Kate could make her hand disappear into them. She pushed the ivy near the ground aside with her sneaker. No baseball.

Kate moved a few feet over. Again, she nudged the ivy back with her foot. This time her toe hit something that moved. She leaned down. It was Mike's baseball!

As Kate straightened up to show Mike the ball, she noticed a big red square on the wall.

"Mike! Mom! Come here quick," she said. "Someone's ripped out the ivy!"

Ballhawks!

Mike, Mr. Thomas, and Mrs. Hopkins ran over to Kate. Ivy blanketed the wall in front of her. But halfway up the wall was an empty spot. No ivy. Just a square of red brick.

"Oh no!" Mr. Thomas grabbed his forehead. "Not again! That's the third time this week."

He leaned over to examine the missing ivy. Someone had neatly clipped away a section of ivy about the size of a baseball glove. The brick wall behind looked like it had been scratched with some type of sharp tool.

Mrs. Hopkins took out her notepad. "What's going on? Who's stealing the ivy?" she asked.

Mr. Thomas shook his head. "I wish I knew. Those scratches make it seem like someone's looking for something," he said. "We've been using green spray paint and extra ivy strands to cover the missing spots. The players are worried it will ruin the Cubs' winning streak if it keeps happening. They get pretty superstitious about things like this."

Mrs. Hopkins flipped her notepad shut. "I've got to get back to the pressroom before the game starts," she said. She handed Kate two tickets. "Here are your tickets. You're sitting just over there, in the right-field bleachers. Mr. Thomas can show you."

Kate's mom waved goodbye. Mr. Thomas led Kate and Mike off the field. They ducked through the door in the outfield wall back to the groundskeepers' room. As he walked, Mike tossed his baseball in an arc in front of him and rushed to catch it. Each time he tried to throw it farther without dropping it.

"Watch this," Mike called to Kate. He tried to toss the baseball in front of him, but it slipped out of his hand. The ball bounced off a workbench.

"Nice one!" Kate said. "Too bad Louie can't help you with your *throws*!"

As Mike was getting his ball, two men and a woman came into the room from the hall-way. The men both had on blue jeans and work boots, but one looked older than the other. The woman had shoulder-length blond hair, and she was wearing a blue Cubs baseball cap and carrying a black backpack.

"Mike and Kate, this is Michael Lee, head groundskeeper," Mr. Thomas said, introduc-ing the older man. "And that's Victor Crumly, his assistant, and Sarah Sampson. She's a college student writing a paper on the history of Wrigley Field."

Sarah and Mr. Lee waved at Kate and Mike. Victor simply nodded and started arranging tools on a nearby workbench.

"Welcome to the *root* of Wrigley Field," Mr. Lee said. "This is where we take care of things from the *grounds* up!"

Mr. Thomas rolled his eyes.

Sarah groaned. She pulled a clipboard from her backpack. "That's so bad I'll have to include it in my Wrigley Field history project."

Mr. Lee snickered a little. "Okay, those puns weren't good, but this *is* where we store all the things we use to take care of the grass," he said, "and the ivy."

"The ivy?" Mike asked. "Kate just found a spot of missing ivy!"

Over by the workbench there was a metallic clattering as something hit the floor. Everyone swiveled to see the source of the sound.

A pair of garden clippers lay on the floor in front of Victor's feet.

"Ah, shoot," Victor said. "Slipped out of my hand."

As Victor bent down to pick them up, his flannel shirt fell open, revealing the T-shirt beneath it. He fumbled around on the floor for the clippers.

Mike's eyes grew wide. He elbowed Kate. "Quick, check out Victor's shirt!" he whispered.

"It's a Chicago White Sox shirt!" she whispered back. "Why's he wearing that? They're the Cubs' biggest rivals!"

Mike nodded. "And did you see the way he dropped the clippers when I said the word *ivy*?"

Victor finally grabbed the clippers and straightened up. "Should we go check on the missing ivy, Mr. Lee?" he asked.

"Yes," Mr. Lee said. "Let's do it now, before batting practice." He tipped his Cubs hat toward Mike and Kate. "Have a good time at the game today!"

After they disappeared through the door, Sarah shook her head. "I can't believe you let a Chicago White Sox fan work on the Cubs' grounds crew," she said to Mr. Thomas. "What if he's the one ripping out the ivy?"

Mr. Thomas shrugged. "Mr. Lee trusts him, so I do, too," he said. "Anyway, we should get going. See you later, Sarah."

Mr. Thomas led Mike and Kate out into the crowded hallway under the bleachers. "You know, batting practice starts in a few minutes. You should take the chance to see the ball-hawks outside the stadium. It's a lot of fun."

Mike's eyes opened wide. "What's a ball-hawk?" he asked. He held up his hands, curled his fingers, and slashed at the air. "That sounds like a giant bird with big *claws*!"

Mr. Thomas laughed. "Not quite. Ballhawks are fans who are really good at catching balls," he said. He opened a door to the street. "See for yourself. Just head over there. You can use your tickets to come back in when you're done."

Mike and Kate thanked him and walked across a blocked-off city street. Fans streamed into the stadium. But a few dozen fans stood on the other side of the street, staring back at Wrigley Field.

"They must be the ballhawks," Kate said. She looked over her shoulder at the outside brick wall of Wrigley Field. Above the wall was the top of the left-field bleachers.

Just then, a ball sailed overhead. It bounced off the sidewalk and over the heads of the fans. The ballhawks made a mad scramble for it.

"I'll bet they're trying to catch home runs that get hit over the wall!" Kate said.

"Let's give it a try!" Mike said. "It would be so cool to catch a Wrigley Field baseball!"

Kate and Mike turned to face the stadium. They crouched down, ready to run in any direction. They didn't have to wait too long.

"Here comes one," someone called.

Kate and Mike scanned the blue sky over the bleachers for the ball. They spied it as it lofted high over the seats.

"There it is!" Mike cried. He ran past a trash can on the corner and down a side street, trying to guess where the ball would drop. Kate followed. She positioned herself about ten feet in front of Mike.

The ball landed right between them. *THWACK!* It shot off the pavement and bounced over Mike's head. A scrum of fans chased it down the street. Finally, a heavyset man in a green T-shirt and shorts held the ball high above his head.

"Wow, this is hard," Mike said. "Those

balls come down really fast. I wish I'd brought my glove."

"There's another one," Kate said.

The ball dropped through the leafy branches of a tree. Mike was just about to snag it when he plowed into a man in a blue shirt and sneakers.

"Ummph!" the man grunted.

The ball bounced off the man's baseball glove. It landed ten feet farther down the road, where a little boy grabbed it.

"Sorry!" Mike said. "You would have had it if I hadn't knocked into you. If I catch one, I'll give it to you."

The man waved his hand. "Thanks, but it only counts if I catch it myself," he said in a gravelly voice. "Besides, I have over four thousand of them at home."

"Four thousand baseballs?" Kate asked. "For real?"

"Catching thousands of balls isn't that unusual for ballhawks," the man said. "I know a lot of ballhawks who have caught over three thousand balls at batting practices and baseball games! Wrigley Field is great because so many balls fly over the bleachers onto Waveland Avenue. We can come to every game and catch balls without even buying a ticket."

"Cool!" Mike said. "I'm Mike and this is Kate. You have any tips for us?"

"Nice to meet you," the man said. "I'm Zack Hampton. The first tip is to pay attention to the fans inside the stadium. You can tell where the ball is going by watching which way they look."

For the next hour, Mike and Kate tried their best to be ballhawks. They chased one ball after another until Mike finally caught one on a bounce. When Kate snagged a ball a few minutes later that flew into a tree trunk, Zack cheered for her. Meanwhile Zack caught three.

A short time later, batting practice ended. Most fans started moving to the stadium gates.

"Got the tickets?" Mike asked Kate.

Kate pulled out the two tickets her mother had given her.

"Thanks for all the help," she said to Zack. "It was great learning how to ballhawk. Too bad you can't give us some help on the missing ivy."

"Oh, the missing ivy," Zack said. He leaned back on his heels and folded his arms across his chest. "People have been talking about that all week. They're worried it will ruin the Cubs' winning streak. It's bad luck when you have strange things happening on your home field."

"I don't know why anyone would want to cut it down," Kate said. "It's so historic."

Zack stroked his chin, deep in thought. "Oh, I think I might know why," he said.

"Why?" Mike and Kate asked at the same time.

Zack glanced around as if he were checking to make sure no one was listening. Then he leaned down and whispered his answer. "Because someone is looking for hidden treasure!"

Bleacher Bums

"Treasure? In Wrigley Field?" Kate asked.

"Like gold bars? Or silver coins?" Mike asked. "We should look for it. If we found it, we could be rich!"

Zack smiled. "Oh, I wouldn't plan on it, Mike," he said. "Just because someone thinks there's treasure under the ivy doesn't mean there is."

"What do you mean?" Kate asked. "Could there really be treasure under the ivy?"

"It's hard to tell. The story started with

Ernie Irving. He was one of the most famous Chicago ballhawks. He used to tell people there was a priceless treasure in Wrigley Field 'under ivy.' But he also said that you'd only find it if you looked under the most important part of Wrigley."

"That *must* be the ivy!" Kate said. "It's the most important part of Wrigley."

Zack held up his hand. "Old Ernie's tale of treasure might not be what you think," he said. "He was a great ballhawk, but he liked to play jokes on people. It's hard to know whether to take his legend of the treasure seriously."

Kate twirled her ponytail around her finger. Then she gave Mike a tug. "Come on, Mike. Let's go to our seats and figure out how to find the treasure," she said. "Thanks for all the ballhawk advice and the treasure tips, Mr. Hampton!"

It didn't take long for Mike and Kate to reach their seats. They were sitting in the first row of Wrigley's right-field bleachers. A thin, grandmotherly woman was next to them. Nearby, fans settled into their seats. They held popcorn, sodas, and hot dogs. The hot dogs were loaded with onions, peppers, mustard, tomatoes, a dill pickle, and the brightest neon-green relish Kate and Mike had ever seen.

At 1:05, the Cubs ran onto the field. Louie Lopez played center field, directly in front of them. The Cincinnati Reds were up first, but the Cubs got off to a great start. Their pitcher, Casey Smit, struck out the first two Reds' batters. The third batter hit a long fly ball down the first-base line. But Ryan Soto, the Cubs' right fielder, ran it down for an easy out. The Reds took the field while Chicago got ready to bat.

Blake Wells approached the plate for

Chicago. Wells was short and stocky, and bat-
ted left. He stood with his feet wide apart and
swirled the bat behind his shoulder. Wells let
two fastballs by for strikes.

"He always swings at the third pitch," the

elderly woman next to Mike said. "And usually he connects!"

She was right. Wells unloaded on the next pitch. The ball flew far into left field. It looked like it would clear the bleachers easily. Then a gust of wind knocked it down, right into the outfielder's glove.

"Drat! It's that wind off Lake Michigan again," the woman said. "Sometimes it blows in. Sometimes it blows out. Keep an eye on those flags on top of the scoreboard to see which way the wind is blowing."

Mike glanced at the scoreboard. A cluster of flags and pennants fluttered at the top.

"You must be new around here," the woman said to Kate and Mike. She had a long, pale face and a nice smile. Curls of gray hair poked out from under an old-fashioned Cubs baseball hat. "I'm Vee Irving. I'm a bleacher bum!"

"You're a hobo?" Mike asked.

Miss Irving laughed. "Oh no, I'm not a real bum," she said. "A bleacher bum is what people call Cubs fans who sit in the bleachers and come to all the games. Around here, it's good to be a bum!"

For the rest of the inning, no Cubs players made it on base. Soon the Reds were up again and the Cubs took the field. As Louie trotted out to center, he spied Mike and Kate. He gave a cheerful wave and then tipped his cap to Miss Irving.

Miss Irving nudged Mike. "He's one of my favorite players," she said. "But he needs to work on his swing!" She pulled out a bright blue pocketbook with a big gold clasp from under her seat. The pocketbook had the initials *I. I.* monogrammed in white thread on its side. Miss Irving opened it and took out a tissue.

"That's a pretty pocketbook," Kate said.

"It was a gift from my father," Miss Irving said. "He told me to keep it under my seat for good luck at every Cubs home game. I've been doing it since I was a little girl. It's a tradition. You know, old Vee Irving and her pocketbook." She snapped the pocketbook shut and slipped it under her seat.

Kate and Mike sat back to enjoy the game. By the eighth inning, the Cubs were ahead 2–1. The Reds had a runner on second and two outs. One of their best hitters came up to bat. On his third swing, he nailed a line drive to the left of second base. The ball shot past Louie, bounced once, and flew straight into the ivy. The runner on second bounded past third. The batter rounded first with dirt flying from his heels.

The fans screamed for Louie to field the ball. Miss Irving jumped up. "Get it! Get it! Get it!" she yelled. Louie leapt to the wall. He scanned the ivy for the ball but couldn't find it. Both runners flew across home plate. Two runs! The Reds were ahead!

Louie turned and held up his hands. The first-base umpire waved the second runner back to second base.

Miss Irving clapped. "Saved by the ivy!"

"What do you mean?" Mike asked.

"The ball got lost in the ivy," Miss Irving said. "According to Wrigley Field's rules, when the fielder can't find the ball in the ivy, it's a double. The second player who ran home will have to go back."

The batter returned to second base. However, something was still wrong. Louie had gone back to rustling around in the ivy. He came out with something in his hand. It wasn't the ball. It was a small hammer with a red wooden handle.

"That's weird," Mike said. "Who left a hammer in the ivy?"

"I don't know," Miss Irving said. "I've never seen that before. Maybe it was the grounds crew."

Kate nudged Mike. "I'll bet it was Victor," she whispered.

Louie handed the hammer to the umpire,

and the game went on. The next batter struck out for the last out. The score was now tied 2–2.

Mike pulled out the baseball he'd snagged on Waveland Avenue before the game. It looked new except for a scuff mark from hitting the street. He held it out for Miss Irving to see. Mike told her how Zack the ballhawk had given them tips on how to catch balls during batting practice.

"My goodness! That's great," Miss Irving said. "My father was one of the first ballhawks at Wrigley Field. He was a huge Cubs fan. You might not believe it, but he caught some of the most famous balls ever hit here. Back in 1932, he snagged a home run hit by Babe Ruth during a World Series game. Have you heard of Babe Ruth's called shot?"

"Sure," Kate said. She knew a lot about baseball history. "That was when the Cubs were heckling Babe. He had two strikes. But then he pointed to center field. He was showing where he was going to hit the ball. He nailed the next pitch clear out of the park for a home run."

"That's right," Miss Irving said. "My father, Ernie, ballhawked it. A few years later, during a 1938 game, he also caught Gabby Hartnett's famous 'Homer in the Gloamin'.' *Gloamin'* means twilight. Hartnett hit a walk-off home run to win the game for the Cubs just as the game was about to be called on account of darkness."

Kate bit her lip and thought. "Did you say your father was Ernie?" she asked. "Is he the Ernie who used to tell people about the treasure hidden in the ivy?"

Miss Irving nodded. "That's right. Ernie was my father. He did like to talk about Wrigley Field's treasure."

"Kate and I are going to try to find the treasure," Mike said. "I'll bet it's silver or gold or something hidden in the outfield wall."

Miss Irving laughed. "That's a fun idea, Mike, but there's no treasure in the wall. My father loved his baseballs and the Cubs, not gold or coins."

The Cubs took the field for the top of the ninth inning. Their three batters had struck out, so the score was still tied.

"I sure hope they win," Miss Irving said. "I'd hate to see our winning streak broken."

The Cubs stayed lucky. The Reds weren't able to score. The Cubs needed just one run to win and keep their streak alive.

Louie Lopez approached home plate. He lifted the baseball bat over his head and stretched his arms back. Then he stepped into the batter's box.

On the second pitch, Louie nailed a fastball right over the plate. He wheeled around and dashed for first. The ball sailed straight toward Chicago's monster scoreboard. Louie rounded first as the center fielder pedaled backward. It was no use. The ball flew over the ivy and sank into the hands of one of the bleacher bums. Home run! The fans exploded with cheers and shouts. Louie and the Cubs had won the game with a walk-off home run!

When the fans settled down, Mike and Kate said goodbye to Miss Irving. On the stairs to the exit, Kate suddenly gave Mike's arm a tug. She pointed to the field. Mr. Lee, the head groundskeeper, was jogging toward the door to the groundskeepers' room in the center-field wall. He had something in his hand.

"He's got the hammer Louie found in the ivy," Kate said. "That gives me an idea."

"Yeah, me too," Mike said. "Like I'm going to hammer in some home runs at batting practice tomorrow, so you better be ready!"

"Hit all the home runs you want," Kate said. "I'll be working on catching."

"Catching?" Mike asked. "I thought we were meeting Louie for *batting* practice."

"We are," Kate said. "But I'm also going to try to *catch* the ivy thief!"

Caught
Green-Handed!

Chicago's early-morning fog was just clearing as Kate, Mike, and Mrs. Hopkins stepped off the red L train at Addison Station. From the platform, they could see the curved back of Wrigley Field's grandstand about a block away. The streets were strangely quiet. Only a few shop workers were around, opening up their stores.

"Remember, we're just staying until lunch, since it's not a game day," Kate's mom said.

"You can go to batting practice with Louie while I'm working. Later, we'll take a tour of Chicago."

Mrs. Hopkins showed her press pass, and they entered through Wrigley's main gate. Maintenance workers were scattered about, cleaning up the stadium and getting the food stands ready. Kate's mother checked her watch. "Let's meet back here at noon."

"Okay, Mom," Kate said. She gave her mom a hug. Then she and Mike headed for the batting cage.

"Do you still think your plan for solving the Wrigley Riddle will work?" Mike asked Kate as soon as they turned the corner.

"Yup. I'm sure it's Victor," Kate said. She ticked off the reasons on her fingers. "He was wearing the White Sox shirt. He dropped the clippers when you mentioned the ivy. And

Miss Irving said a groundskeeper might have put that hammer in the wall."

"And he just seems suspicious," Mike added. "I didn't like the way he looked at us."

As they neared the batting cage, Kate and Mike heard the *PLONK* of Louie's bat hitting ball after ball. The sound echoed off the cement block walls.

Mike's jaw dropped when the batting cage came into view on the left side of a wide hallway. "This is awesome!" he said. They were under the right-field bleachers.

Large windows stretched from the ceiling to down near the floor. Mike and Kate watched as a trainer threw balls to Louie from behind a screen. A huge black net hung from the ceiling. It captured the balls Louie hit.

When Louie saw Kate and Mike waving through the windows, he winked at them. Mike counted as Louie took thirty more pitches. He hit some line drives that flew straight past the trainer's screen. A few hit the metal edges, making a loud *TONK* sound.

Finally, Louie motioned for the kids to come in. They entered through a big glass door in the middle and wound around the netting to the other side. Mike lifted the edge, and they ducked under it into the batting cage.

"*¡Hola, amigos!* You ready to hit some out of the park?" Louie asked. When Mike and Kate nodded, Louie handed Kate his bat. He had her grip it a few inches up the handle. "If you choke up on the bat, you'll be able to swing faster."

Kate slipped on a batting helmet and walked over to the plate at the end of the batting cage. She bent her knees and held the bat up behind her shoulder. It wavered, and she tried to hold it steady. Mike and Louie stepped to the other

side of the netting to watch. Kate nodded at the trainer behind the screen, and he tossed the first ball.

Kate swung hard. But she missed, and the ball sailed over the plate. She choked up a little more and nodded to the trainer again. He fired the next ball. Kate swung hard again. This time she connected. The ball flew right past the trainer's screen into the back of the net. Louie and Mike cheered.

"*¡Bueno!*" Louie said. "I don't need to give you any pointers!"

Kate smiled and waved for the next pitch. She hit one after another. She only missed when the trainer tried some tricky pitches. Soon it was Mike's turn. He wasn't as lucky as Kate. He fouled off most of the pitches above or behind him. But he did make a few high pop-up hits.

"Looks like you're trying to golf, not play baseball," Louie called out. "Swing the bat level!"

After about ten swings, Louie stepped back in and told Mike to open up his stance and swing earlier. It made a huge difference. After that, Mike hit a lot of solid line drives and some grounders.

When it was time to stop, Kate and Mike thanked Louie. "That was great," Kate said. "I can't believe we got to have batting practice at Wrigley Field."

"*De nada*—it was nothing," Louie said. "I'll make sure to tell my manager I've found some new prospects! If we keep having close games like yesterday, we might need your help. We need to improve our hitting, or we'll definitely blow the winning streak."

Mike gave Kate a high five. "All right!" he said. "We'll be back in the bleachers tomorrow if he needs to find us! Right next to Miss Irving."

Louie chuckled. "Oh yeah. Miss Irving and her big blue pocketbook," he said. "I see her at every home game. Old Ivy Irving sure is a *great* fan. But I wouldn't mind if she stopped telling me how to bat!"

"Well, she does know a lot about baseball," Kate offered. "She also seems to like you."

"Maybe she's right," Louie said. "I'll go practice a bit more. You can tell her I was working on my swing for her." Louie winked and headed back to the batting cage.

"Come on!" Kate whispered to Mike. She pointed to the exit. "Now's our chance!"

Out in the hallway, Kate and Mike passed food shops and stands until they reached the groundskeepers' room. Kate cracked open the door. "It's empty," she whispered.

Rakes, shovels, hoses, and bags of grass seed leaned against walls or lay on the dark blue concrete floor. It was hard to tell where to start.

"We might not have much time, so let's try to find that hammer," Kate said. "I'll bet Mr.

Lee brought it here after the game. He probably put it on the workbench. I'll look there. You look behind those bags and hoses."

Mike checked out the bags stacked against the side wall. He slid a few of them apart to see if there was anything underneath. There wasn't. When he lifted up a pile of coiled hoses, all he found was a puddle of water.

Kate wasn't having much luck at the workbench, either. On top was a jumble of tools. She was just about to give up when Mike came over.

"There's nothing over there," he said. "Did you find the hammer?"

Kate's ponytail bobbed back and forth as she shook her head. "Nope, no sign of it."

Mike started rustling around with the tools on the workbench. He pushed one pile of tools all the way to the left. Then he picked through them, checking one at a time.

"Hey, be careful!" Kate said. "We're not supposed to be messing with the tools!"

"It's got to be here somewhere!" Mike said. "We saw Mr. Lee bring it back after the game." He continued moving items from the left side of the workbench to the right.

"Aha!" Mike said. He grabbed a wooden handle sticking out from the pile but bumped into Kate as he did. She lost her balance and knocked into a big white plastic bucket. The bucket's top popped off.

"Watch it, you moose!" Kate said. She gave him a pinch. "Don't worry, I'll fix it." She scurried to put the top back on the bucket.

"Good!" Mike said. "While you're fixing that, I'll be finding a clue!" He pulled a hammer from the pile of tools. It had a heavy head and a smooth wooden handle. At the end of the handle was a band of red paint and a small red metal ring to hang it on the wall.

Kate's eyes grew wide. "That's the hammer Louie found in the wall during the game!" she said. "And guess what? It matches perfectly with what I just found!"

Kate pulled a trowel and a chisel from the big plastic bucket. They both had red paint and red metal rings on their handles. Just like the hammer.

"I'll bet Victor's using this bucket of tools to hunt for the treasure!" Kate said.

Before Mike could answer, they heard a metallic scrape.

"That's the door to the field," Kate said. "We've got to get out of here!"

Kate dropped the tools and put the top of the bucket back on. Then she jumped for the door to the hallway. But Mike, who tried to head in the other direction, ran right into her. By the time they untangled themselves, a figure loomed in front of them.

"What are you two doing snooping around here?" the man said. "This area is off-limits to visitors!"

Mike and Kate looked up.

It was Mr. Lee. He held a pair of clippers in his right hand.

Kate thought fast. "We had batting practice with Louie," she said. "And we were thirsty, so we were looking for a drink."

Mike nodded. He swallowed and pointed to his throat. "It's dry," he squeaked.

"But we were just about to—to—to—" Kate stammered as she stared at Mr. Lee. "We were about to—"

Mike followed Kate's eyes. She was staring at Mr. Lee's left hand. He had pulled it out from behind his back.

Mike's jaw dropped.

Mr. Lee held a huge bunch of ivy!

"You're the ivy thief!" Mike shouted.

The Ivy Thief

"We've solved the Wrigley Riddle!" Kate said.

Mr. Lee glanced at the ivy strands in his hand. Then he started laughing. "Me? You're kidding, right?"

Kate dug her heel into the ground. Mike crossed his arms. They both stared back at Mr. Lee.

Mr. Lee shook his head. "I'm not the ivy thief," he said. He put the clippers on the workbench and pulled out a can of green spray paint from the pocket of his pants.

"More ivy was destroyed last night. I was out there covering the brick wall where the ivy is missing," he said. "I used the clippers to clean up some damaged vines. That's why I have these." He shook the clump of ivy in his left hand. "You've got the wrong person. I'd love to catch the thief just as much as you would!"

Kate leaned forward. "Well, then, who do you think the thief is?" she asked.

"That's a great question," Mr. Lee said. "We put in security cameras to try to catch the ivy thief. But somehow they got turned off, so nothing was recorded."

"What about your assistant, Victor?" Mike asked. "Does he know anything?"

"I'm not sure," Mr. Lee admitted. "Victor called in sick this morning. I haven't had a chance to talk to him." He put the spray paint and ivy vines down on the workbench.

Mike exchanged a look with Kate. Before he could ask any more questions, the door to the field creaked open. The blond woman from the day before walked in.

"Oh, hello, Sarah," Mr. Lee said. "You're in early. What are you working on today?"

"The scoreboard," she answered. "I want to take pictures and write notes for my research."

"Have fun," Mr. Lee said. "We have one of the most unusual scoreboards in baseball!"

"Are you actually going up in the scoreboard?" Mike asked.

Sarah nodded. "Would you like to come along? I'd be happy to show it to you, if it's okay with Mr. Lee."

"Really? We'd love to!" Mike said. He looked at Mr. Lee.

"It's fine with me," Mr. Lee said. "Just be careful climbing the ladder."

"I'll be sure to watch them," Sarah said.

She led Mike and Kate out into the hallway and up the ramps to the bleacher level. The stadium was empty except for a few workers. Soon they were standing directly below the huge metal scoreboard.

Sarah climbed the rungs of the skinny metal ladder. She used her key to unlock a trapdoor in the bottom of the scoreboard. Mike and Kate followed her inside.

"Wow! It's a lot bigger in here than I thought," Mike said after he stood up. Metal beams and stairs surrounded them.

"It's three stories tall," said Sarah. "And there's even another ladder that goes to the roof. They use that to change the flags on top of the scoreboard. If the Cubs win, they raise a white flag with a *W* on it."

Rows and rows of big white zeros filled the

wall at the front of the scoreboard. "Hey, what are all those zeros?" Mike asked.

Sarah laughed. "That's the back of the scoreboard," she said. "Let me show you." She led them past a table covered with large green metal squares. Each square had a white

number painted on it. In front of the table sat two chairs facing the field.

"This is where workers hang the scores for all the baseball games," Sarah said. "From the stands, the scores from National League games are on the left. The ones from the American League are on the right. During a game up to four people can be in here, keeping track of all the numbers and scores."

Sarah showed them how the metal squares slipped into special holders in the front wall, like pictures into frames. When she took one out, Mike and Kate had a great view of the field.

Kate peeked through the empty number slot. Shadows of clouds moved across the out-field. She nudged Mike. "This would be the perfect place to hide overnight to try to catch Victor ripping out the ivy!" she whispered.

Sarah pointed to two round metal fans on

the floor. "They need those because it gets pretty hot in here during a day game in the summer," she said.

"But it's still a pretty *cool* place to watch a game," Mike chimed in. Kate laughed and shook her head.

Sarah unzipped her backpack and took out her clipboard and a camera. "The only parts of the scoreboard that aren't manual are the big clock on the top and the electronic numbers for balls, strikes, the batter, and outs," she said. "Those are controlled by the scorers in the press box. I can show you a picture."

She pushed some buttons on her camera. Then she held up the display screen for Kate and Mike to see. Sarah scrolled through pictures of the front of the scoreboard. She showed them pictures of the clock and the lights that marked balls and strikes.

Sarah flipped past the scoreboard pictures to ones of the outfield wall. The first pictures showed the outfield wall with green ivy everywhere, except for a big square in the center of the brick.

"Oh, sorry," Sarah said. "Went too far." She pressed the "back" button to return to the scoreboard pictures. "That was for my work."

"Do you know anything about the missing ivy?" Kate asked. "We heard that someone was looking for treasure under it."

"I heard that, too," Sarah said. She looked around to make sure no one else was listening. "Can you keep a secret?"

Mike and Kate nodded. "Sure," Kate said.

"I'm trying to trap the ivy thief," she said. "That's why I was taking notes earlier. I have good reason to believe it's Victor, the grounds-keeper's assistant!"

"So do we!" Mike said. "He was acting funny before!"

"That's why I'm watching him," Sarah said. "But he won't find any treasure."

Mike looked at her in surprise. "He won't?"

"Nope. I know something about it that no one else does," she said as she slipped the camera into her backpack. "I found an old newspaper article that said that one of the old ballhawks just made up the story. There's no gold or silver in the wall. The Wrigley Field treasure is a hoax!"

Mike's Big Idea

The elevator doors slid shut. "Hold tight! In just a few moments you'll be at the top of the highest building in America," a prerecorded voice said. "For now, just watch the numbers on the red display above the door count up to one hundred and three. That's right, you're going up a hundred and three floors!"

Mike and Kate felt their knees buckle a little as the elevator car rocketed to the top of the building. Mrs. Hopkins leaned against the back wall and held her stomach.

"If there's no treasure like Sarah said, what do we do?" Mike asked Kate.

Kate watched the numbers zoom past the twenties, thirties, and forties.

"It actually doesn't matter if there's treasure or not. If Victor's a White Sox fan, he could be damaging the ivy to ruin the Cubs' winning streak," Kate said.

"You're right!" Mike said. "If we catch him, we can still solve the Wrigley Riddle."

The elevator slowed to a halt.

Mike grabbed the side of his head. "Ouch! My ear hurts!"

Mrs. Hopkins held out a couple of pieces of blue bubble gum. "It's just from going up so high so fast," she said. "Try chewing this gum. It should help."

Mike and Kate both took a piece of gum and popped it into their mouths. As the elevator doors opened, Mike's face broke into a wide grin. "My ear just popped! I can hear again." To celebrate, he blew a big blue bubble.

"That's good," Kate's mom said, nudging Mike forward. "Then maybe you can hear the tour guides asking you to exit the elevator!"

Mike popped his bubble and sucked the gum back into his mouth. Then he stepped off the elevator onto the observation deck of the tallest building in America. A sunlit view of Chicago and Lake Michigan spread out around him.

Mike and Kate ran to the nearest window. Way below stood a bunch of tall buildings. They could see the green grass of Grant Park. Beyond that lay the beaches and blue water of Lake Michigan. The windows facing south showed a completely different scene. Mike and Kate could see the Chicago River winding between buildings and train yards.

But the side facing west was the cool-est. Instead of just windows, it had four big, clear glass boxes that jutted from the side of the building. Each was about eight feet wide, eight feet tall, and four feet deep. And each had a *clear glass floor* that looked straight down 103 stories!

"We're supposed to walk on them?" Mike asked.

Kate pulled him gently onto the glass ledge. "See, it's not that bad," she said. "It's really strong." Mike glanced through the glass under his feet. It felt like he was standing on air. More than 1,300 feet below, moving people and cars looked like ants.

Then he heard Kate calling. She was standing back on the central floor. "Hey, Mike," she said. "Watch this!" Kate sprinted toward him.

Mike held up his hands. "What are you doing? Are you crazy?" But it was too late. Kate took a flying jump from the floor. She sailed toward the glass ledge.

THUD! Kate landed on the glass right in front of Mike. The floor shook. But it didn't crack. It didn't break. And they didn't fall 103 stories to the city street below.

"I can't believe you did that!" Mike said. "What if this thing broke?"

Kate smiled and shook her head. "There's no way. It's made to be super-strong," she said. "I read about it in the guidebook last night."

When they finished trying to count the tiny cars below, Mike and Kate went over to the windows facing north. Nearby, two workers cleaned the glass.

"Wrigley Field is out there somewhere," Mike said. He blew a small bubble with his gum and pointed to an area with lots of brick buildings and trees.

"I don't think we can see it without binoculars," Kate said.

"What if we set a trap for Victor?" Mike asked, thinking about the missing ivy again.

"What kind of trap?" Kate asked.

Mike bit his lower lip and thought. "We just

need to figure out what he's going to do before he does it."

Kate laughed. "Oh, that's easy. Thanks for the good idea!" she said.

They spent a few more minutes trying to pick out other Chicago landmarks and then looked for Kate's mom.

A few feet over, the window washers were also finishing up. Mike watched as they placed their tools into a big white plastic bucket.

"That's just like the bucket we found yesterday," Mike said.

"You mean *I* found," Kate said.

"Whatever," Mike said, rolling his eyes. "I'll bet Victor's using those tools to search for the treasure."

Kate nodded. "But how does that help us?" she asked. "We can't stay at the stadium all night and watch the bucket."

"No, we can't," he said. "But I've got a better idea!"

Mike chewed his gum for a minute and then
puckered his mouth. He blew a huge bubble.
After a few seconds, he popped it with his finger and folded it back into his mouth.

"We'll set a trap with gum!" he said.

A Ring of Gum

Kate popped a chunk of bright blue gum into her mouth. Then she handed one to Mike. "Here, have another," she whispered. "We need to make sure we have enough."

Mike's cheek was already bulging. He slipped the new piece into his mouth. "I'm not sure I can chew any more pieces," he said.

"We have to get as much ready as we can," Kate said, chewing away. "We won't have a lot of time once we get there."

They had just pulled up in a taxi outside

Wrigley Field. Kate had convinced her mom they needed to go back to check the batting cage for Mike's baseball. She said they had left it behind during batting practice.

Mrs. Hopkins showed her press pass to the security guard, and they entered the empty stadium.

"When you're done, meet me at the press office," Kate's mom said as she headed down the corridor. "I'll get some work done while you're looking."

"'Oooodbye,'" Mike mumbled through his wad of gum.

"'Aaaterrrrr,'" Kate said, trying to avoid choking on her own mouthful.

They ran down the corridor on the first-base side of the empty stadium, past bathrooms and stairs. They passed the batting cage area under the bleachers and stopped in front of the groundskeepers' room. Through the hallway windows, they could see the workbench with the tools and all the piles of equipment lying nearby.

"'Ood. 'O one is 'ere," Kate said, drooling slightly. She wiped her chin with the back of her hand. She looked up and down the hallway. Since it was close to five o'clock on a day when there was no game, the bleachers were empty.

Mike pushed the door open. Only the utility lights were on, so the room was in shadow. A few feet over from the outfield door stood the white plastic bucket. The top was securely on.

"'Eady?" Kate garbled through her gum.

"'Eady," Mike said. After looking around one more time, they both started to pull long, thin strands of sticky gum from their mouths. When they had a strand as long as their arms, they draped it on the floor around the bucket.

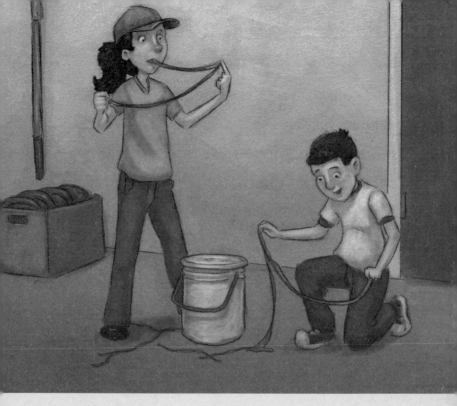

Soon strands of dark blue gum ringed the bucket. The gum blended in perfectly with the dark blue of the floor.

"Looks good!" Kate said. "Let's get out of here!"

Mike nodded.

They quietly slinked back to the hallway.

The trap was set!

The next morning, Mike and Kate pushed against the crowds of people near Wrigley Field's entrance. Kate's mom had an important phone call that ran late, so they didn't make it to the stadium until just before batting practice.

The ticket taker scanned Kate's and Mike's tickets and waved them in. They sprinted straight to the groundskeepers' room under the bleachers.

"It might not have worked," Kate said. "What if Victor wasn't here last night?"

"I'll bet it did," Mike said. "I can just feel it!"

Kate pushed open the door to the workroom. They were in luck. The room was empty. Mike and Kate ran over to the bucket. They both leaned down to look at the rings of gum around the bucket.

Kate shook her head. "I can't believe it," she said.

"I can't, either," Mike said. "It worked!"

He was right. In several places, the gum was pressed flat, as if someone had stepped in it. When Mike and Kate looked more closely, they even spotted a little trail of gum leading to the door in the outfield wall.

"Victor must have come in last night and opened the bucket," Mike said. "I'll bet he got some tools to look for the ivy treasure!"

Then Kate noticed something even more interesting. She pointed to a spot with a large blob of gum. "There's a tread mark in the gum!" she said. Four or five little circle patterns had been pressed into the center of the blob.

"It's like a stamp!" Mike said. "Now all we have to do is match this pattern with the one on Victor's shoe. We can prove he's cutting down the ivy!"

Mike and Kate were still leaning over the

gum when the workroom door swung open. It was Victor!

"What are you two doing here?" he asked.

"Ah, we were just, um, looking for something," Mike said.

"Yeah, like who stole the ivy!" Kate said.

Victor glared at them. He was about to say something when Mr. Lee walked in.

Mr. Lee glanced at Mike and Kate, and then at Victor. "Well, what's going on here?" he asked. "Is there a problem?"

Victor pointed at Kate and Mike. "These two kids are sneaking around where they shouldn't be," he said. "They're not allowed in this area."

Kate stepped forward. "I know," she said. "But we were just following clues to the missing ivy!"

"Clues that prove he did it!" Mike said, pointing at Victor. "He's been coming in here at night

80

and using tools from that bucket to search for treasure. Just check his shoes!"

Mr. Lee turned to Victor. He seemed as confused as Victor did.

"Why would we look at Victor's shoes?" Mr. Lee asked.

Kate showed Mr. Lee how she and Mike had spread the blue gum around the bucket. She also pointed out the trails of gum leading to the outfield and the little circle patterns pressed into the gum.

"His shoes will prove he did it!" Mike said.

Victor shook his head. "This is crazy," he said.

Mr. Lee examined the gum on the floor. "Maybe we should just take a peek at your shoes, Victor," he said.

"I can't believe this," Victor said. "You think I'd cut down the ivy?"

"Let's just take a quick look at those shoes to be sure," Mr. Lee said.

Victor hung his head and lifted up his right sneaker. Mike, Kate, and Mr. Lee leaned in to get a better look.

Victor's sneakers had tread marks. But the treads were large, wavy lines. Not little circles.

Mr. Lee straightened up. "Well, I guess that answers that question," he said. "Thanks, Victor. You can get on with your work now."

"But he had a White Sox T-shirt on the other day," Mike said. "He's a White Sox fan and wants to ruin the Cubs' winning streak!"

Victor stared at Mike for a moment and then he snickered. "I wear a *White Sox* T-shirt when I'm scheduled to do *dirty* jobs around the stadium. Even Mr. Lee knows that!" he said.

"Maybe he wore a different pair of shoes!" Mike tried, but Mr. Lee was shaking his head.

"It's not Victor," he said.

Across the room, the door to the hallway opened. The noise of fans for that afternoon's game grew louder as Sarah Sampson stepped inside.

"Hi, everyone," she said. "Just dropping off my stuff." She leaned her black backpack against the wall. Near the door, Victor started coiling piles of water hoses.

"I can't believe it," Mike whispered to Kate. "It had to be him!"

"I know," Kate said, tugging at her ponytail. "The gum trap was such a great idea."

Sarah was rummaging through her backpack. All of a sudden, there was a clunk and her clipboard dropped to the floor. As Sarah knelt down to pick it up, something blue caught Mike's eye.

Mike squinted at Sarah's sneakers. She crouched in front of her backpack and the soles of her shoes faced the room.

"Look, the bottoms of her sneakers have tiny circles all over them," Mike said. "And blue gum! Sarah's the ivy thief!"

Two Home Runs

Mr. Lee looked at the bottoms of Sarah's shoes. The pattern matched the prints in the gum near the bucket exactly. Blue strands of gum were even still stuck to her shoes, along with red clay from the warning track.

Sarah spun around and stood up. "Wh-what are you talking about?" she stammered. "I don't have anything to do with the missing ivy."

"We set a gum trap, and you're the one we caught!" Mike said.

"Check her camera, too!" Kate said. "I didn't think about it then, but yesterday Sarah showed us some pictures by mistake that she had taken of the missing ivy. There's a shot of the ivy she cut lying on the ground."

Mr. Lee flipped through the pictures on the camera. "I have to admit, all the clues suggest you did it," he said. "What do you have to say for yourself, Sarah?"

Sarah's shoulders slumped. "I'm sorry," she said. "I lost my college funding and don't have enough money to go back to school. I needed to find that treasure so I could stay in college!"

"I'm afraid we'll have to take you to the security office," Mr. Lee said. He picked up Sarah's backpack and led her away.

"Nice work," said Victor from the other side of the room. He had been watching them the whole time.

"Thanks," said Kate. She blushed. "Sorry we thought it was you. The White Sox shirt had us fooled."

"It's okay," Victor said. "But if you don't get to your seats soon, you'll miss today's game!"

"Come on, then," Mike said, tugging Kate's elbow. "Let's go!"

Mike and Kate pushed through the door into the hallway. Mike led the way to the same bleacher seats as yesterday. On the field, players stretched and ran sprints.

"Hello again," Miss Irving said from her same spot. "Just in time for the game."

Kate stepped into the row first. "You'll never believe what happened. We just caught the person stealing the ivy!" She went on to explain how she and Mike set a gum trap and how Sarah had walked right into it.

"That's wonderful!" said Miss Irving. "It's

too bad Sarah was doing terrible things to our ivy. You two are so smart. My father, Ernie, would have loved what you did. He would have said that you deserve a reward!"

Miss Irving fished around for her pocket-book under her seat. She finally found the strap and lifted up the big blue pocketbook. Sunlight glinted off the gold clasp.

"My father used to give me a silver dollar when I did something good," Miss Irving said. "I suppose those don't buy much anymore, but they're still pretty neat."

Miss Irving popped the clasp open and pulled out two big, old-fashioned silver dollars. She gave one to Mike and one to Kate.

"Wow! Cool!" Mike said. The front of the shiny silver coin had an image of President Eisenhower and the date 1972. The back showed an eagle landing on the moon. "See, Kate! I told

you we'd get some treasure! Thanks so much,
Miss Irving."

Kate held her coin in her hand. Mike had
said the treasure would be silver coins. And
there they were!

The game started. The Cubs ran out to take
the field. Louie Lopez was in center field again.
He waved to Mike, Kate, and Miss Irving.

That made Kate think of something Louie had said. Her eyes went to the side of Miss Irving's pocketbook. The letters *I. I.* stood out on the blue cloth. Kate's heart beat faster.

"Miss Irving, we took batting practice with Louie yesterday," Kate said. "He told us to tell you that he would work on his swing. But he also said something else."

"Oh, that's nice . . . ," Miss Irving said. "I do so like Mr. Lopez."

"When he was talking about you, he called you Ivy Irving. Not Vee, like you told us," Kate said. "Is your first name Ivy?" She held her breath.

Miss Irving laughed. "Yes, it is. But most people call me Vee."

Kate let out a soft whistle and grabbed Mike's arm. "I think we've just found the treasure!" she whispered to him.

Mike's eyes opened wide. "We have?" he asked.

"It's been right here all the time," Kate said.

"Where?" Mike asked. "In the bleachers?"

Kate gripped the edge of her seat. She turned back to Miss Irving. "I figured it out!" she said. "The silver coins under your seat! They're the treasure under the ivy!"

"What's that?" Miss Irving asked. "What do you mean?"

Kate smiled. "Your father told everyone there was a special treasure in Wrigley Field, hidden under ivy. When he said *ivy,* he meant his daughter, Ivy, not the ivy on the wall. And when he said *treasure,* he was talking about something in your pocketbook. Your pocketbook is always under Ivy at Wrigley Field! Your silver dollars—they are the treasure!"

Miss Irving's eyes crinkled up as she

91

smiled. She started to say something, but Kate kept going.

"Your father said the treasure was hidden under the most important thing in Wrigley Field. Most people think that means the ivy is the most important thing. But I think your father meant the *fans*. The treasure is really hidden under the fans—like you!" Kate said.

Miss Irving didn't answer Kate. Instead, she set her blue pocketbook in her lap. She pulled out a tissue and wiped a tear from her eye.

"I've been thinking about this moment for years," Miss Irving said. "I've always wondered who would be smart enough to finally figure out my father's riddle. I'm so glad it's someone as nice as you two!"

Her face broke into a big smile as she unsnapped the golden clasp on the pocketbook. "You're right about my treasure. But you got one thing wrong," she said to Kate. "The silver dollars aren't the treasure. This is."

Mike and Kate both leaned forward and held their breath.

Miss Irving took two old-fashioned baseballs in clear plastic cases from the pocketbook. She handed one to Kate and one to Mike.

"They're the special home run balls that my father ballhawked here at Wrigley Field," Miss Irving said. "He told me to bring them to every game. I kept them under my seat for good luck."

Kate and Mike turned the plastic cases over in their hands. The balls inside were brown and worn. They weren't nearly as shiny or smooth as a new one.

Miss Irving pointed to Kate's baseball. "That's the home run ball that Gabby Hartnett hit for the 'homer in the gloamin','" said Miss Irving. Then she pointed to the ball in Mike's

hand. "That one is the ball Babe Ruth hit for the 'called shot.'"

"Wowee!" Mike whistled. "These must be worth a million dollars!"

Out on the field, it didn't take long for the Cubs to get ahead of the New York Mets. By the fifth inning, the Cubs were winning 6–2. Louie Lopez even hit one more run in the eighth inning to make the final score 7–2.

After the game, Kate and Mike signaled to Louie. He came over to the outfield wall, and Ivy showed him the baseballs. Louie told them he'd send Mr. Thomas out to talk with Miss Irving. As he turned to go, Louie gave a thumbs-up to Kate and Mike, and two thumbs-ups to Miss Irving!

A short while later, after Mr. Thomas had stopped by, Kate's mother joined Miss Irving, Kate, and Mike in the bleachers.

"Mom! Look at what Miss Irving had," Kate said. She showed the priceless baseballs to her mother and told her their history.

Mrs. Hopkins examined the two baseballs.

"These are amazing," she said. "What a real treasure!"

Miss Irving smiled. "Now that the Cubs are on a winning streak, it's a good time to give the baseballs a new home," she said. "As you guessed, my father always said the real treasure at Wrigley Field was the fans. He'd be happy to know that his baseballs are finally going to be shared with all baseball fans."

Kate held up the shiny plastic case with the Gabby Hartnett ball. "She's giving this one to the Cubs. They're going to build a big display case in the main entrance so everyone can see the ball," Kate said. "Mr. Thomas says it'll bring good luck to the Cubs. Enough good luck for them to win the World Series this year!"

Mike tugged at Mrs. Hopkins's sleeve. "And Miss Irving is going to give the Babe Ruth ball to the National Baseball Hall of Fame in Cooperstown," he said. "That means we can see it whenever we want, since it will be just down the block from our homes!"

Dugout Notes
☆ Wrigley Field ☆

Ivy. One of the most famous things about Wrigley Field is the ivy on the brick outfield wall. P. K. Wrigley had ivy installed in 1937 to cover the brick. On opening day each spring, the ivy vines are bare and brown. By summer, they grow thick green leaves. The ivy looks soft, but it doesn't provide much padding. Outfielders have to be careful not to slam into the wall.

"The Friendly Confines." Wrigley Field's nickname is the Friendly Confines because the ballpark is small and the fans are friendly. It's the second-oldest ballpark (after Fenway Park in Boston).

Flags. Flags and pennants are all over Wrigley Field. When the Cubs win a game, a white flag with a *W* is raised over the center-field scoreboard. If they lose, a blue flag with an *L* goes up.

Lights. In 1988, Wrigley Field became the last major-league ballpark to get lights for night games. They were supposed to be installed during World War II, but the Cubs donated the lights to the war effort. Until 1988, all games at Wrigley Field were played during the day, even on weekdays. Unlike most teams, the Cubs still play many of their games during the day, even though they have lights.

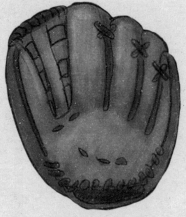

Bleacher Bums. Because Cubs games used to be played only during the day, fans who wanted to watch a game during the week had to take a day off from work or school. Since the fans weren't at work, they earned the nickname "bums" or "bleacher bums."

Lovable Losers. The Chicago Cubs have had a lot of heartbreak over the years. Although they won the World Series in 1907 and 1908, they've gone more than a hundred years without another World Series win. Even though the Cubs always seem to lose at the wrong time, the fans are loyal and love their team.

Gum. William Wrigley Jr. founded a company in 1891 to sell soap and baking powder. To help sales, he included chewing gum with his products. But when the gum became more popular than the products, he started selling the gum by itself. The Wm. Wrigley Jr. Company still sells gum today. After he made a lot of money selling gum, Mr. Wrigley bought the Chicago Cubs, and after he died, his son, P. K. Wrigley, ran the Cubs.

Billy Goat Curse. The Chicago Cubs have lost a lot of important games over the years. Some fans believe it's because of the Billy Goat Curse. In 1945, the owner of the Billy Goat Tavern tried to bring his pet goat to a World Series game. But he was told to leave the stadium because his goat was too smelly! People say that when he was on his way out, he cursed the Cubs, say-ing they'd never win a World Series again because the team insulted his goat.

Rooftops. Wrigley Field is in the middle of the city. In fact, the top floors of the apartment buildings on the streets behind the outfield walls overlook the field. That meant some fans could watch the games from the nearby rooftops without buying a ticket! Many of the buildings have recently installed rooftop bleachers. Now fans can buy tickets to see the game from *inside* the stadium or *outside* the stadium!

Ballhawks. Before each game, dozens of ballhawks gather outside Wrigley's left-field wall on Waveland Avenue. They hope to catch one of the home runs hit during batting practice or games. But Wrigley

Field is also important because on April 29, 1916, it became the first major-league stadium to allow fans to keep home run balls hit into the stands. Before that, fans had to toss the balls back to the umpires!

Throwing It Back. Cubs fans don't like when the other team hits a home run. They have a tradition of throwing home run balls from the other team back onto the field!